Gulliver's Travels

Jonathan Swift

Artist: Penko Gelev

First edition for North America (including Canada and Mexico), Philippine Islands, and Puerto Rico published in 2009 by Barron's Educational Series, Inc.

© The Salariya Book Company Limited 2009

All inquiries should be addressed to:
Barron's Educational Series, Inc.
250 Wireless Boulevard
Hauppauge, New York 11788
www.barronseduc.com

ISBN-13 (Hardcover): 978-0-7641-6245-9
ISBN-10 (Hardcover): 0-7641-6245-4
ISBN-13 (Paperback): 978-0-7641-4280-2
ISBN-10 (Paperback): 0-7641-4280-1

Library of Congress Control No.: 2008939082

Picture credits: Topfoto.co.uk

Every effort has been made to trace copyright holders. The Salariya Book Company apologizes for any omissions and would be pleased, in such cases, to add an acknowledgment in future editions.

Printed and bound in China.
Printed on paper from sustainable sources.
9 8 7 6 5 4 3 2 1

Gulliver's Travels

Jonathan Swift

Illustrated by

Penko Gelev

Retold by

John Malam

Series created and designed by

David Salariya

The monkey took me up in his right forefoot and held me as a nurse does a child … And when I offered to struggle, he squeezed me so hard, that I thought it more prudent to submit. I have good reason to believe that he took me for a young one of his own species, by his often stroking my face very gently with his paw.

(see page 17)

CHARACTERS

Lemuel Gulliver

Emperor of Lilliput

Empress of Lilliput

Flimnap

Reldresal

Skyresh Bolgolam

Emperor of Blefuscu

King and Queen of Brobdingnag

The Farmer

Glumdalclitch

Laputians

King of Laputa

Lord Munodi

The Academy Projector

A Struldbrugg

Gulliver's master,
a Houyhnhnm

A Yahoo

VOYAGE TO LILLIPUT

Bristol, England, May 4, 1699.

I hope our journey shall be prosperous.[1]

I am Lemuel Gulliver, a doctor and failed businessman. Some time ago I decided to leave England, so I took work as a ship's doctor aboard the *Antelope*.

Six months later...

We reached the South Sea.[2] But the ship sank, and only I survived. I was washed up on a distant island that I later learned was Lilliput.

Who are you?

I awoke to find myself tied to the ground. I was surrounded by tiny people, no more than six inches high.

Tolgo phonac![3]

As I tried to free myself, one of them shouted in Lilliputian. The others shot tiny arrows at me!

Hekinah degul![4]

I lay still until the attack stopped. I felt hungry, so I pointed to my mouth. The clever Lilliputians brought me food and drink.

That night, 900 people put me on a specially built carriage and took me to their capital city.

I was taken to a temple, which I could fit inside if I lay down. There my left leg was chained up and locked with 36 padlocks. I was a prisoner.

1. prosperous: successful.   2. South Sea: the name given by early explorers to all oceans south of the equator.
3. Tolgo phonac, and 4. Hekinah degul: Gulliver doesn't tell us what these words mean.

THE EMPEROR'S PRISONER

The surrounding countryside was very pretty. The Emperor of Lilliput visited, but neither of us spoke the other's language, so their greatest scholars were brought in to teach me theirs.

A staff of 20 brought carts of food and drink to me every morning, prepared by 300 cooks—enough to feed 1,728 Lilliputians per day!

Crowds of people came to stare at me. Six men, whom I took to be troublemakers, fired arrows at my face. One of their arrows very narrowly missed my eye.

I scooped the men up and pretended I was going to eat one of them. But I had no intention of causing him harm, so I put all the men down. My act of mercy was praised, but I was still kept in chains.

One day, I was entertained with a display of rope-dancing. Two threads were stretched out high above the ground, and two men climbed up. The Emperor commanded them to dance.

I watched, as Flimnap, Treasurer of Lilliput, and Reldresal, Secretary of Private Affairs, balanced and jumped on the threads. I was told that the man who jumped highest would receive the best job.

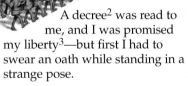

I am the Emperor's Colossus![1]

Do not let him go.

At a council meeting, officials discussed whether to release me from my chains. Only Skyresh Bolgolam, the High Admiral, wanted to keep me locked up.

GOLBASTO MOMAREN EVLAME GURDILO SHEFIN MULLY ULLY GUE, most Mighty Emperor of Lilliput, Delight and Terror of the Universe, whose dominions extend five thousand blustrugs [about twelve miles in circumference] to the extremities of the globe; Monarch of all Monarchs, taller than the Sons of Men; whose feet press down to the center, and

Golbasto Momaren Evlame...

A decree[2] was read to me, and I was promised my liberty[3]—but first I had to swear an oath while standing in a strange pose.

You will be very useful to me.

I bowed and promised to help the Emperor defeat his enemies. I was free at last.

He is a Man-Mountain!

1. Colossus: giant statue.
2. decree: an offical announcement.
3. liberty: freedom.

Gulliver Saves Lilliput

I believe five hundred thousand souls live in Mildendo.

I visited Mildendo, the capital of Lilliput. For their own safety, the townsfolk stayed inside their houses.

The two mighty powers are engaged in a most obstinate[1] war.

Reldresal, who had become my friend, told me that Lilliput was threatened with invasion by its enemy, the country of Blefuscu.

The war had begun when a Lilliputian Prince had opened an egg at the large end and had cut his finger.

You must obey the law.

The prince's father made a law saying that eggs must only be opened at the narrow end.

We will open our eggs at the big end!

But many people objected to the law. Eleven thousand Lilliputians were killed in the rebellions that followed.

"All true believers shall break their eggs at the convenient end."

The rebels, called Big-Endians, fled across the sea to Blefuscu. The Blefuscudians took their side in the struggle.

The Blefuscudians declared that Lilliput had broken a law in the Blundecral, the holy book.

Lilliput and Blefuscu could not agree on the "convenient end" of an egg. Now the Blefuscudians were planning to invade Lilliput.

1. obstinate: stubborn, unwilling to give in.

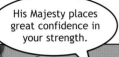

His Majesty places great confidence in your strength.

The purpose of Reldresal's visit became clear—the Emperor wanted me to join the fight against the Blefuscudians. I agreed to defend Lilliput from the invaders.

I waded across the sea to the Blefuscudians' warships. Many of the enemy jumped ship. Others shot at me with arrows, but I ignored them. I tied the ships together, then cut their anchor cables.

Long live the most puissant[2] Emperor of Lilliput!

With great ease, I drew fifty of the enemy's largest men-of-war[1] back with me to Lilliput.

I will not bring a free and brave people into slavery.

I bid you[3] destroy all Big-Endians.

The Emperor then commanded me to help him take control of Blefuscu.

But I plainly protested. I would not be used for this purpose.

My refusal to help clearly angered him, and he never forgave me.

1. men-of-war: warships.
2. puissant: powerful, strong, mighty.
3. bid you: ask you to.

UNDER SENTENCE OF DEATH

I am content to gratify[1] the curious reader with some general ideas of Lilliput.

The Lilliputians believe the world is flat and will, in time, be turned upside down. Therefore, they bury their dead upside down.

When the world turns upside down, the dead will come back to life. They will rise from the ground head first and standing up.

Children are not raised by their parents. Instead, they are sent to live in nurseries, where they learn to be adults.

There are separate nurseries for boys and girls. Children wear plain clothes and eat simple food.

Parents see their children for one hour, twice a year. They can kiss their children once, but bringing toys or sweets is forbidden.

People think more of you than they do Skyresh Bolgolam.

One night, an official told me in secret that since I had taken the Blefuscudian ships, Skyresh Bolgolam had become my enemy.

Skyresh Bolgolam has called for your execution.

He showed me a list of crimes I was charged with. Refusing to conquer[2] Blefuscu for the Emperor was one of them.

Skyresh planned to kill me by setting fire to my house.

12   1. content to gratify: would like to entertain.   2. conquer: to defeat someone through overwhelming force.

Reldresal defended me, saying that my life should be spared, and that I should be blinded instead.

It was agreed that I should be blinded but, in addition, my food would be reduced.

I was to be sentenced in three days' time, but as I valued my eyesight, I decided to leave Lilliput. I seized one of the Emperor's ships and escaped to Blefuscu.

I went to the capital city of Blefuscu, and was met there by the Emperor and Empress. They welcomed me to their land.

Three days after arriving, I saw a rowing boat in the sea. It had come from a wrecked ship.

With the help of 3,000 men, I pulled the boat ashore. The Emperor gave permission for it to be made ready to sail.

The Emperor of Lilliput sent a message demanding my return, but the Emperor of Blefuscu refused.

A month later, I began my journey home. I took food for the voyage, plus six cows and two bulls, and the same number of sheep and rams.

By good fortune, I was rescued by an English ship. Back at home, I sold the miniature animals for a handsome profit. But soon I longed to travel again.

Voyage to Brobdingnag

June 20, 1702.

Some months later, I began a new voyage.

Brobdingnag, June 16, 1703.

Don't go far.

I wish to see this country.

I sailed on the *Adventure*, bound for the East Indies. After a year at sea, a large island was sighted. We stopped to collect water.

Finding nothing of interest, I started back, only to see the men fleeing, pursued by a giant!

I am a Lilliputian in this world.

I was all alone in this strange place, and ran for my life. I came to a field of barley, with stalks 40 feet high. The corn was being cut by a huge creature.

Stop!

I was almost cut in two by the giant's reaping hook.[1]

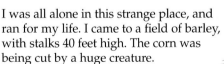

Aah! You are pinching my sides!

The giant lifted me 60 feet into the air. He stared at me with great curiosity, then tucked me into his lapel[2] and ran to his master.

He showed me to the farmer, who blew on my face and jabbed at me with a piece of straw.

The farmer put me down and placed a handkerchief on his hand. I bowed and lay down. He carried me away, gently wrapped up.

1. reaping hook: a tool with a sharp, curved blade used for harvesting crops.
14   2. lapel: the folded collar of a coat.

I was taken to the farmer's house. At first, his wife screamed at the sight of me. But she was soon reconciled,[1] so I ate with the farmer's family.

I was tired and so was put to bed. I awoke to find two hugh rats sniffing me! I fought them off with my hanger,[3] killing one of them.

The farmer's daughter, whom I called Glumdalclitch, made me a bed from a drawer.

News that the farmer had found a strange animal spread. An old friend of his came to inspect me, and gave the farmer an idea.

At next market day, the farmer put me in a box and we rode into town. Glumdalclitch came too.

There, I was made to entertain the crowds—again and again—with a pretend sword fight. I felt half dead with tiredness.

Among the crowd was a mischievous schoolboy, who launched a hazelnut at my head. Had it hit me, it would have knocked my brains out! The young rogue was quickly dragged away.

August 17, 1703.

Thinking that I was to make him a fortune, the farmer set off with myself and Glumdalclitch for Lorbrulgrud, the capital city. Its name means "Pride of the Universe."

1. reconciled: calmed.   2. mastiff: a large breed of dog.   3. hanger: a type of sword.
4. Grildrig: a made-up word which roughly means "mannikin" or "dwarf."
5. splacknuck: an imaginary tiny creature, about 7 inches long.

GIANT DANGERS

> Would you be content to live at court?

> Yes, but I am my master's slave.

> Surely this is a piece of clockwork—a toy.

The farmer showed me ten times a day. I grew so weak I almost became a skeleton. He took me to see the Queen of Brobdingnag.

I was sold to the Queen for one thousand gold coins. Glumdalclitch came with me as my nurse.

I was taken to the King, who asked me many questions. To his delight, I answered them all, in the language of Brobdingnag.

> It is like a bedroom in London.

> Tell me of Europe and its customs.

> Come here, you ant!

A cabinet-maker built a box in which I could live. It had padded walls to protect me if the room were dropped, and a lock to keep rats out.

Every Wednesday I dined at the King's table. The Queen's dwarf joined us, and took pleasure in seeing a creature smaller than he.

One day, this malicious[1] urchin dropped me into a bowl of cream and left me there to drown.

I was also attacked by twenty wasps, of which I killed four.

> It is the strangest creature!

Fortunately, Glumdalclitch fished me out. The dwarf was given a severe beating, and was made to drink the bowl of cream.

I wanted to explore, so I went into Lorbrulgrud with Glumdalclitch. She showed me the houses and the people.

16 1. malicious: spiteful, mean.

Malicious rogue!

A dog snatched me in the same garden.

Another time, Glumdalclitch took me into the royal garden. The Queen's dwarf shook an apple tree, and huge apples came tumbling down around me.

The dog took me to its master. I was out of breath and could not speak, but was unhurt.

He has such skill!

The Queen, who liked hearing about my sea voyages, ordered a boat to be made for me. A water tank was built for me, and she watched as I rowed to and fro.

The greatest danger I ever faced was when a monkey ran off with me and climbed a roof. Fortunately, I was rescued by a servant boy.

SEEKING LIBERTY

I entertained the King and Queen with an English tune which I played upon the spinet.[1]

How hard he works for our amusement.

The worst race of little odious vermin that Nature ever suffered to crawl upon the surface of the Earth.

Twenty or thirty cannon will destroy the town of your enemy.

On many occasions the King asked me to describe the people and customs of my country. After much thought, he told me what he thought of the English.

I tried to change his low opinion by telling him about the great discovery of gunpowder. I informed his majesty that I knew how to make it, and could instruct his workmen how to make cannons.

I would rather lose half my kingdom than learn such a secret.

But the King was horrified. He was amazed that an insect (that is what he called me) could be so cruel, and he forbade me from mentioning it again.

I found the King—and all Brobdingnagians—to have narrow minds.[2] I was curious to know more, and set about learning all I could by reading their books, especially those about history and customs.

---

1. spinet: an early form of piano.
2. Gulliver seems to think the King's reaction to violence is narrow-minded, something that most modern-day readers would disagree with. However, Gulliver's own opinions of violence seem to change later on (see page 33 onward).

18

"I long to walk among fields without fear of being trod to death like a frog."

Two years went by while I toured the kingdom with the royal family.

I yearned to see the ocean again, so one day a pageboy carried my travelling box down to the seashore.

"He will pick out my body for a meal!"

I asked to be set down. As I gazed out upon the sea, the boy went off to look for birds' eggs.

Suddenly, my box was moved with great force high into the air. It was gripped by an eagle, who carried it far across the ocean.

England, 1706.

"You should never go to sea again."

The great bird dropped me into the sea. Luckily, I was found by a European ship bound for England. I arrived home nine months later.

After four years at sea, my wife was pleased to see me. But I was so used to the company of giants that, when around humans, I stooped to make myself feel small.

THE ISLAND IN THE SKY

August 5, 1706.

I had been home only ten days when a captain asked me on a new voyage. With permission from my wife, I happily accepted.

I was made master of a sloop[1] bound for China, but my ship was caught by two pirate vessels.

We will cast you adrift.

The pirates ransacked my ship and took my men, while a pirate crew took charge of my sloop. My fate was in their hands.

Having put me in a small boat, the pirates sailed away, taking my ship as their prize. Once again, I was at the mercy of the sea.

An island!

I reached an island, which I later learned was Balnibarbi. I survived by eating birds' eggs.

What is that curious sight?

Five days later…

I spied a vast body[2] passing in front of the sun. I looked through my pocket-perspective[3] and could see people moving about on it, so I called out as loudly as I could.

1. sloop: a small, fast sailing ship.
2. body: object.
3. perspective: telescope.

Where am I going to?

I have no need of such an instrument.

A chain was let down from the flying island and I was pulled up. I was met by a crowd of very strange beings, whose heads leaned either right or left and whose eyes looked in opposite directions. Many of them seemed distracted and deep in thought.

These Laputians are obsessed with music.[3]

I was taken to the King of Laputa. On either side of him was a flapper holding a flap.[1] It was the Laputians' custom to be "flapped"[2] when speaking or listening, otherwise they would forget what they were talking about.

A room was prepared for me, and servants brought me food shaped like musical instruments. Later, the King sent a teacher, so that I could learn Laputian.

The King gave orders to fly over the towns of Balnibarbi. Ropes were let down, and the townsfolk tied petitions[4] to the ends, which were then pulled up to Laputa.

I noted how superstitious the townsfolk seemed. They spent much time gazing at the sky and observing the sun. They thought that one day the sun would stop shining over Balnibarbi.

1. flap: a stick with an inflated balloon filled with dried peas or little pebbles.   2. flapped: touched with a flap on the ears and mouth.   3. obsessed with music: the Laputians are obsessed with mathematics, and in Swift's time, music was considered to be a form of mathematics.   4. petition: a request for something to be done.

EXPLORING THE ISLANDS

I must now inform the reader about the curiosities of Laputa, which measures 4.5 miles across.

At the center of the island is the Astronomers' Cave.

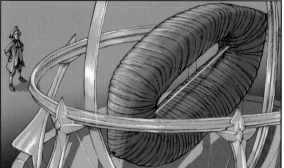

The astronomers here spend their lives observing the sky. They have studied 10,000 stars and 93 comets, and have discovered two moons around the planet Mars.

The greatest curiosity, upon which all of Laputa depends, is the lodestone.[1] It is the power of this giant magnet that allows the island to rise and fall, float and move. The lodestone is in the care of certain astronomers.

Should a town on Balnibarbi threaten to rebel against Laputa, the King has ways of punishing it. For a mild punishment he might move Laputa so that it blots out sunlight over the town.

For a severe punishment, boulders are dropped onto the buildings.

1. lodestone: a natural magnet.

"I am heartily weary of these Laputians."

The ultimate punishment is when Laputa itself settles on a town, crushing everything beneath it. This was tried on the rebellious town of Lindalino.

But the townsfolk of Lindalino had built towers filled with magnets, which upset Laputa's lodestone. Fearing a crash, the King gave in to the Lindalinians.

Having seen all I wished of Laputa, I was anxious to visit the island of Balnibarbi.

"These people follow modern, scientific methods of farming."

"Why are there no crops? The soil is excellent."

I descended as I had arrived.

I was shown around the island by Lord Munodi, who had once been the governor of Lagado, the capital of Balnibarbi. I was struck by its poverty. The people wore rags and lived in hovels. They were plowing fields in the most unproductive way.

"I use traditional methods of farming."

"He is old and weak..."

"...and cannot manage his affairs!"

Lord Munodi then took me to his estate in the country. While the Balnibarbians grew no food, Munodi's grand house was surrounded by vineyards and fields of golden wheat.

The Balnibarbians made fun of Lord Munodi. They thought his traditional methods set a poor example as to how the kingdom should be managed.[1]

1. Swift believed that new ideas in 17th century politics and science were often ineffective, and his descriptions of the Balnibarbians seem to reflect this.

A VISIT TO THE ACADEMY

The Academy, Lagado.

I visited the Academy, where scientists known as projectors[1] worked. Lord Munodi thought their experiments were futile[2] and that they had let the country go to waste.

A projector told me he had spent eight years trying to extract sunbeams from cucumbers, but had run out of money for his experiments.

Another projector showed me his device for turning ice into gunpowder. It was the strangest experiment, and the scientist had met with no success.

There was a blind projector who employed several blind assistants. They mixed colors for artists to paint with. They identified the colors by touch and smell, but they were not very good at their lessons.

One projector had found a new way of plowing fields—burying acorns in neat rows, then letting pigs dig them up. He hadn't realized that it was as much trouble to sow the acorns as it was to plow the land.

1. projector: when Swift was writing, a projector was a person who formed wild or impractical ideas.
2. futile: hopeless, useless.

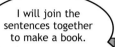

I will join the sentences together to make a book.

I was shown a machine that wrote books. As students turned its handles, a pattern of words appeared. When the words seemed to make part of a sentence, it was written down. Then books were made from these broken sentences.

I witnessed a student eating a wafer[1] with sums written on it.

My pupils eat nothing but bread for three days afterward.

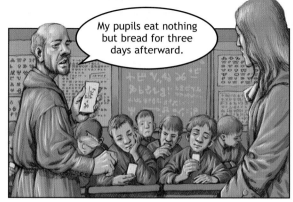

The mathematics projector explained that as the wafer was digested, the sum supposedly rose into the brain. But the rebellious students made themselves sick before the wafer had been properly digested.

A pinch a day prevents forgetfulness.

A medical projector told me of his method for improving the memory—a pinch on the nose or a kick in the belly!

Men should pay the most tax.

Women should be taxed according to their beauty.

I listened to a strange debate between two projectors on the subject of tax.

It is time to return to England. But how?

After visiting the Academy, I came to the conclusion that Balnibarbi had nothing to offer me. My thoughts turned to a more pressing matter.

1. wafer: a thin, crisp cracker.

TALKING WITH THE DEAD

I hired donkeys and a guide, and was taken to the port of Maldonada, on the south coast of Balnibarbi. I hoped to find a ship bound for the island of Luggnagg, from where I could sail to Japan and then home.

But none of the ships were sailing to Luggnagg, so I decided to board a vessel to Glubbdubdrib, the Island of Magicians.

On Glubbdubdrib I met the governor who, with a snap of his fingers, could summon the dead to work as his servants.

They serve me for twenty-four hours, after which I call for new servants.

I have never seen such magic!

Another snap and they vanish.

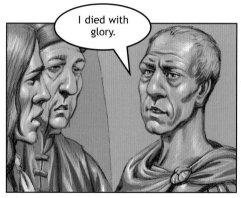

The governor said I could name anyone from history to appear before me, and that I could command them to answer my questions. They had to answer truthfully. I first called on Alexander the Great.[1]

Then I summoned the Roman general Julius Caesar.[2] He first appeared with his troops, whom he was leading into battle, and later I had the honor of talking to him about his life and death.

I summoned the Greek poet Homer.[3] He did not think much of the governor.

I called on many other ancient writers and thinkers.

It occurred to me that I could introduce spirits from different times to each other, so that they could discuss their ideas.

I saw most of the first emperors of ancient Rome, and called on Roman cooks to prepare us a dinner. They could not show us many of their skills, as it was hard to find the ingredients they needed.

Finally, I called on the spirits of the recently dead, and from them I learned the truth about modern history. What they said shocked me deeply.

1. Alexander the Great (356–323 B.C.): an ancient Greek military leader.   2. Julius Caesar (c.100–44 B.C.): an ancient Roman military and political leader.   3. Homer: an ancient Greek writer, who lived around 750 B.C.
4. Aristotle (384–322 B.C.): an ancient Greek philosopher.   5. Descartes (1596–1650): a French philosopher, mathematician, and scientist.

AMONG THE IMMORTALS

April 21, 1709.

On Lugnagg…

Two weeks later…

I had seen all I wanted of Glubbdubdrib and its spirits, so I resumed my voyage to Luggnagg.

I told an official of my plans to sail home. I was taken to a house, where I was to stay until I gained permission to leave the country.

The officer took me to the King of Luggnagg. An interpreter travelled with me, as I did not speak their language.

I must have many enemies here.

I was granted permission to lick the dust before the King's footstool, as was the custom. The floor was swept clean as I was a stranger, but if I had been considered an enemy, the floor would have been sprinkled with dirt.

Ickpling gloffthrobb squutserumm blhiop Mlashnalt Zwin…[1]

Fluft drin yalerick dwuldom prastrad mirpush.[2]

As instructed, I touched my forehead seven times to the ground and spoke in the King's language. After this, I used the language of Balnibarbi, which my interpreter translated into the language of Luggnagg.

1. Ickpling…: "May your celestial Majesty outlive the sun, eleven moons and a half."
2. Fluft…: "My tongue is in the mouth of my friend." (Gulliver is explaining that he needs a translator.)

While on Luggnagg I learned of the Struldbruggs, or immortals.[1] On rare occasions an immortal was born, with a red spot above its left eye. As the child grew, the spot's color changed, until it was black and changed no more.

If I were immortal, I would be the richest man in the kingdom.

My property was given away.

Being immortal is a form of living death.

Spare a token for an old man?

I learned the problems of being a Struldbrugg. At 80, the law treats them as dead.

They lose their hair and teeth and forget people's names, even those of their friends. I met a 200-year-old Struldbrugg who had become a beggar.

I decided that I had no wish to live forever if it meant living like these poor people.

May 12, 1709.

We will give you all the help you require.

I bring with me this letter of introduction.

April 10, 1710.

I had seen enough of Luggnagg, so I boarded a ship to Japan from the island's main port.

After fifteen days, I was in Japan. I presented a letter from the King of Luggnagg, which was given to the Japanese Emperor.

I was taken to Nangasac, Japan, and boarded a ship to Holland. From there I sailed to England. I reached my house on April 11, 1710.

1. immortals: people who live forever.

LAND OF THE TALKING HORSES

I decided to return to sea. I was captain of the *Adventure*, with orders to trade in the South Sea.

During the voyage, my crew caught calentures—a fever that made them think the sea was a green field. They tried to jump onto it, but drowned.

Try to escape and we'll shoot you.

I stopped in the West Indies for new men, but found out too late they were pirates. They seized my ship and held me prisoner.

May 9, 1711.

The pirates set me ashore on an unknown island. They wanted to be rid of me.

Cows, people... and many horses.

I have never beheld in all my travels so disagreeable an animal.

Walking about the island I came to a path. Trod into its surface were animal tracks.

Exploring further, I saw several animals, which I later learned were Yahoos. Some were squatting on the ground, others were climbing trees.

Stay away from me!

One Yahoo came toward me. It raised its paw and, thinking it was about to attack me, I struck it with the flat of my dagger. It roared, and the herd of the ugly creatures surrounded me.

What has frightened them away?

I ran from the creatures but they caught up with me. All I could do was wave my dagger at them to keep them away. Then, in the middle of my distress, the Yahoos suddenly scattered.

I have good cause to believe you can understand me.

Are these metamorphosed[1] magicians?

The Yahoos had been startled by two horses. They came to me and touched me with their hooves, which they used like hands.

I listened to them neighing, and it seemed they were talking. I heard them say "Yahoo" many times, and then their own name, which was "Houyhnhnm."[2]

The Houyhnhnms led me to a house.

Yahoo!

I bring knives, bracelets, necklaces, and a mirror for your master.

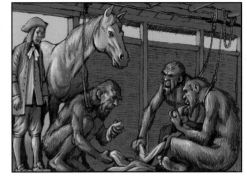

Inside were five Houyhnhnms, sitting on their haunches, not eating as horses do in a stable, but engaged in conversation. I offered gifts to their master.

The gray[3] led me to a small building. Inside were three Yahoos, tied up by their necks. They were feeding on roots and the flesh of donkeys, dogs, and diseased cattle.

The smell is awful.

I came from over the sea in a great vessel made of the bodies of trees.[4]

The Houyhnhnms compared me with a Yahoo and offered me raw meat. But I turned away and the Yahoo ate it up.

For their food, the Houyhnhnms ate oats. I mixed some with milk, and made bread for me to eat.

After about three months with the Houyhnhnms I had learned enough of their language to tell them I was not a Yahoo.

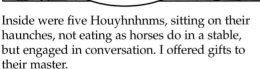

1. metamorphosed: transformed.   2: Houyhnhnm: this word represents the neighing of a horse.
3. gray: gray or white horse.   4. a great vessel…: Gulliver is talking about his ship.

A Description of England

I regarded the gray as my master. I explained to him that in my country it was creatures like me (whom he thought of as Yahoos) who were the governing animals, not the other way around.

Horses were used by farmers and carriers, who had them pull carts to transport their goods. These horses were treated with kindness, until they became lame or too old to be useful.

I explained about the uses of a saddle, a bridle,[2] a spur,[3] and a whip. I added that we fastened shoes of iron to horses' feet, to preserve their hooves.

My home, I said, was an island far away called England. The country was governed by a queen. I told him I was a surgeon, and had left England to travel in search of riches.

1. presiding: ruling, leading. 2. bridle: a head harness used to control horses.
3. spur: a spike or spiked wheel worn on a rider's heel, designed to encourage a horse to go faster.
4. Queen Anne (1665–1714) was the real Queen of England at the time when the story is set.

I spoke about wars, telling him that during England's long war with France, about one million of my fellows had been killed. My master said that the Yahoo's (or human's) vile nature was to blame for such violence.

I told him about our systems of law. I explained how lawyers argued that black is white and white is black.[1] He thought it a great pity they could not put their skills to better use.

I told him that humans are naturally greedy.

The rich get richer by making the poor work for them. The bulk of our people are poor, and are forced to live in poverty.

Englishmen drink wine from other countries, not because we lack water, but because wine makes us merry and raises our hopes.

Our sick are cared for by doctors who claim to understand the nature of disease. They say they are skilled in the use of medicine and can restore a patient to good health.

These same doctors are guilty of killing the sick. It is as if they have the power of predicting death. The truth is, they cannot cure the sick. Their medicines do more harm than good.[2]

1. black is white and white is black: Gulliver means that they went in for pointless arguments.
2. more harm than good: Many 17th- and 18th-century medicines were ineffective and sometimes led to death.

33

THE YAHOOS

I found the Houyhnhnms to be creatures of the utmost virtue[1] and understanding.

My master sent for me and commanded me to sit down. He said he had thought long and hard about my whole story. He told me what he had decided and compared me with the Yahoos.

It was obvious, he said, that I did not have the strength or agility of my brethren,[2] as he called them. I could not run with them, nor climb trees as they did. They collect shining stones, just as humans covet[3] wealth.

In the same way that humans get drunk on wine, Yahoos suck the juice from a root. It makes them do strange things, until they fall asleep in the dirt.

Sometimes a Yahoo crawls into a corner and howls. The only way to bring it to its senses is to set it to hard work—something that humans dislike.

1. virtue: moral goodness.
2. brethren: brothers (the Yahoos).
3. covet: desire, wish for.

I felt I needed to understand human nature better than my master, and so I decided to spend time among the Yahoos. I once caught a young Yahoo, which screamed and scratched, and smelled terrible.

Yahoos live in burrows which they dig with their hands. They eat roots and herbs, and search for carrion,[1] or sometimes catch weasels and wild rats, which they greedily devour.

From the day they are born, Yahoos swim as well as frogs. They hold their breath for a long time and catch fish. Their masters, the Houyhnhnms, are everything the Yahoos are not—kind and friendly.

The Houyhnhnms train their young to be strong and fast. They exercise by running up and down steep hills and over stony ground.

Every four years the Houyhnhnm leaders hold a Grand Assembly. The Assembly was held to discuss whether to keep or kill the Yahoos.[2] My master spoke in favor of keeping them.

1. carrion: the flesh of a dead animal.
2. The Yahoos are kept like slaves, something that Gulliver (and perhaps Swift) does not object to. Unfortunately, slavery was legal and common when Swift was writing, which may explain why Gulliver does not seem at all bothered about the Yahoos' welfare.

A Sad Farewell

I stayed with the Houyhnhnms for three years.

Necessity is the mother of invention.

I became very settled. My master had ordered a house to be built for me, and I made it as comfortable as I could. When my clothes were worn to rags, I made new ones from rabbit skins, and shoes from Yahoo skin.

I lived simply, with few comforts. I often got honey out of hollow trees. By mixing it with water, I could make a sweet drink, which I drank with my bread.

We would like to ask your Yahoo some questions.

Some Houyhnhnms were curious but wary of me.

I cannot bear the sight of myself.

I do not know how you are going to take this news.

When I thought of my family and friends, I thought of them as Yahoos disguised as humans. I turned away in disgust if I happened to glimpse my reflection.

One day, my master informed me that the General Assembly had discussed me, and had taken offense at his keeping a Yahoo (meaning myself) in his family home. They said he treated me more like a Houyhnhnm than a brute animal.

Some Houyhnhnms thought that I should be treated the same as the other Yahoos, but others feared I might lead them into rebellion. Instead, the General Assembly ordered that I was to be sent away.

On hearing the news, I was overcome with grief and despair. I fainted, and fell to the ground at my master's feet. I came to my senses after a while, and my master said he thought the news had killed me. I said I could not swim home—I needed a boat.

I was given two months to make a boat. I made the frame from oak, which I covered with the skins of Yahoos. When it was finished it was pulled down to the sea.

On the day of my departure, I said farewell to my master and I kissed his hoof. Then, getting into my canoe, I pushed off from the shore and paddled away from the land of the talking horses.

1. Hnuy illa…: "Take care of thyself, gentle Yahoo."

HOME TO ENGLAND

February 15, 1714.

I began my desperate voyage at nine o'clock in the morning. I sailed all day, and at around six I spied a small rocky island where I spent the night.

The next day I set off again, and after seven hours I reached New Holland.[1] For three days I fed off raw oysters and limpets. On the fourth I was found by a group of natives, who wanted my canoe.

The natives fired an arrow and it struck me in the knee. I paddled out to sea, where I pulled the arrow from my leg and dressed the wound as best I could.

Who are you?

I am a poor Yahoo who has been banished from the Houyhnhnms.

I saw a ship, but I had no desire to be taken by European Yahoos, so I paddled away and returned to New Holland. But a boat came to collect water, and I was discovered. The sailors thought I neighed like a horse.

He has such civilities[2] for a Yahoo.

You are welcome to sail with us.

I was taken on board the ship, which was a Portuguese vessel on its way home to Lisbon. We reached Lisbon on November 5, 1715.

1. New Holland was the name given to Australia by European sailors.
2. civilities: manners, kindness.

December 5, 1715.

We thought you were dead!

They seem like odious animals to me.

After some weeks, I boarded a ship to England. At last I arrived at my house. I had been away for five years.

My wife and family were overjoyed to see me. I did not feel the same toward them—my time among the Houyhnhnms had caused me to think of the human race as no better than vile Yahoos.

My spirits are revived at the sight of you.

For the first year after my return I could not bear to be in the presence of my family. I detested the smell of humans, and I much preferred the company of my two horses.

Gentle reader, I have given you a faithful history of my travels for sixteen years.

For the rest of my life I will apply the lessons I learned from the wise and thoughtful Houyhnhnms.

39

THE END

JONATHAN SWIFT (1667–1745)

Jonathan Swift was born on November 30, 1667 in Dublin, Ireland. His father died a few months before Jonathan was born, leaving his mother to raise Jonathan on her own. Instead, she handed him over to a nursemaid, who raised him in the town of Whitehaven, a busy port on the northwest coast of England.

EDUCATION IN IRELAND

Swift's nursemaid treated him as if he were her own son. At the age of 3 he was able to spell and read, and was returned to his mother in Dublin. But before long his mother left Ireland and went to stay with her own family in England. Swift stayed in Dublin, and from then on his uncle Godwin (his father's brother) took charge of him.

Godwin made sure that Swift received a good education. Between the ages of 6 and 14 he attended Kilkenny Grammar School. It was a boarding school about 70 miles (112 km) southeast of Dublin, and was the best school in Ireland. In later life, Swift wrote about his time at Kilkenny, saying it was a place of "delicious holidays," "charming custards," "ten hours a day to nouns and verbs," "the rod" (the cane used to beat pupils), "bloody noses" and "broken shins." Swift left Kilkenny when he was 14 and went to Trinity College, Dublin, to study Latin, Greek, Hebrew, and philosophy. He was there for six years.

A 19th-century portrait of Jonathan Swift.

SWIFT THE WRITER

Jonathan Swift is best known for his satirical novels—works of fiction that were sometimes serious, sometimes funny, but were always critical of people and the society they lived in.

Swift began his writing career in his early twenties. At first he wrote poetry, but soon he began to write political pamphlets, which were short essays that discussed important issues of the day. He went on to write full-length books. His most famous book, now known as *Gulliver's Travels*, took several years to write, and was published in 1726 as *Travels into Several Remote Nations of the World*. The author's name was given as "Lemuel Gulliver." The book became an instant success, and within a year it had been translated into French, German, and Dutch. It was the only book for which Swift ever received any money—£200 for the manuscript.

SWIFT THE PRIEST

Swift left Trinity College in 1689. It was a time of unrest in Ireland, and Swift was among many people affected by changes in the country. He felt it was best to leave Ireland, and so he travelled to England in search of work. In his early twenties he started his first job as a secretary (private assistant) to a wealthy man. It was not what he really wanted to do, so in 1690 he travelled back to Ireland. In 1695 he became a priest in the Church of Ireland, working in the village of Kilroot, near Belfast. In 1700, he settled in Laracor, near Dublin, where he continued his work as a priest. Then, in 1713, he became Dean of St. Patrick's Cathedral, Dublin. He kept this job for the next thirty years, almost to the end of his life, but it is not as a clergyman that Jonathan Swift is remembered.

MADE-UP NAMES

Swift rarely used his own name in his writings. Instead, he either used no name at all (the author was anonymous), or he used a made-up name (a pseudonym). He used the pseudonym "Lemuel Gulliver" for *Gulliver's Travels* for two reasons. First, he wanted his readers to think it was a true story—an exciting adventure about new lands. He wrote from the point of view of Gulliver (a first-person narrative) because he wanted his readers to think that Lemuel Gulliver was a real person describing events that had actually happened.

The second reason Swift used a pseudonym was for his own safety. In 1724 Swift wrote a series of pamphlets called the *The Drapier's Letters*, which criticized England's involvement in Ireland. Swift used the pseudonym "M. B. Drapier" to protect himself against the angry response the pamphlets received—one wealthy Englishman offered a reward of £300 for the real name of the author.

In *Gulliver's Travels*, Swift uses satire to criticize people in authority, such as politicians, doctors, and lawyers. He uses Gulliver and his experiences to poke fun at English society. However, because the book was so popular, Swift admitted that he was the author as soon as *Gulliver's Travels* was published, and he quickly became famous.

FINAL YEARS

When Swift was 23 he began to suffer from Menière's disease—a disease of the inner ear which he said sounded like "the noise of seven watermills." It afflicted him for the rest of his life, causing him to feel dizzy and sick. When he was in his early 70s he started to become forgetful and confused, and in 1742 he was declared "unsound of mind." In 1745, Swift died at age 78. He was buried in St. Patrick's Cathedral, Dublin.

Gulliver's Travels is one of those rare books that have never been out of print. When it was released in 1726, it caused a sensation. It's a work of satire, which is a style of writing that uses humor and exaggeration to point out people's weaknesses. People understood the criticisms that Swift was making about the society he lived in. Now, more than 275 years later, it's much harder for us to understand. In fact, it has been described as one of the "most misread books." The following descriptions outline some of the key points that Swift was making.

LILLIPUT (1699–1702)

In his first adventure, Gulliver meets a race of tiny people—the Lilliputians. Swift uses them to reveal the very worst side of human nature. The Lilliputians are petty and cruel, just as humans can be. The individual Lilliputians described by Swift represented some of the leading politicians of the day, and the book's readers would have soon worked out who was who. For example, Swift based Flimnap, the Treasurer of Lilliput, on Robert Walpole (1676–1745). Walpole dominated British politics in the early 1700s, and is regarded as the first British prime minister.

When Swift described the bizarre rope-dancing contest between Flimnap and Reldresal, he was making a point. At first sight it seems to be something out of a circus act, but why should two high-ranking Lilliputians be made to perform tricks for the Emperor? Swift is comparing politicians with acrobats.

He's saying that if politicians want to get better jobs, they have to perform pleasing tricks for their leader.

Swift thought that politicians could not be trusted. One minute they might be friendly, the next minute they could be your enemy. Swift uses the Emperor of Lilliput to make this point. We see the Emperor turn against Gulliver and sentence him to death because Gulliver refuses to do something he disagrees with. Gulliver is described as bigger and better than the Lilliputians (in other words, the politicians of Britain).

BROBDINGNAG (1702–1706)

Gulliver's second adventure takes him to a race of giants—the Brobdingnagians. Now it's Gulliver's turn to feel small, while all around him are people who are physically bigger than he is, and who have better morals (standards) than he does. In Lilliput, Gulliver was the giant, but on Brobdingnag he is made to feel as insignificant and as worthless as an ant. Seen through Gulliver's eyes, everything is larger than life. Swift does this to magnify human weakness and folly (stupidity). For example, in his conversations with the king, Gulliver offers to give him the secret of gunpowder. Gulliver imagines the king will be pleased. But the king is horrified at the thought of having such a terrible weapon. Because of this, Gulliver decides the Brobdingnagians, despite their great size, have small minds. But, perhaps the opposite is true, and Swift is telling his readers that it's

Gulliver who is the stupid one. Surely, only a person who lacks morals would seek to harm others through violent acts? In putting Gulliver among giants, Swift makes a powerful point about the real world—the biggest man is the one who shuns violence, and who settles an argument peacefully.

LAPUTA AND BALNIBARBI (1706–1710)

Gulliver's third adventure takes place on two islands—Laputa and Balnibarbi. Laputa is a flying island that hovers above the island of Balnibarbi. On Balnibarbi, Gulliver discovers a race of beings who are preoccupied with what he considers to be useless activities, although they have convinced themselves that they are great scientists. Their experiments never work, but the scientists don't know that and they carry on regardless.

In Swift's time, many scientists and philosophers (thinkers) were trying to bring an end to centuries of superstition and out-of-date ideas, and set the stage for something new. Some people find changes to their routines and ways of life very hard to live with. Others see change as their opportunity to improve their lives. Perhaps the Balnibarbians were not really the "mad scientists" that Swift makes them out to be. Instead, they can be interpreted as modern, free-thinking men.

LAND OF THE TALKING HORSES (1710–1715)

Gulliver's last adventure is perhaps the oddest of all. He finds himself among talking horses (the Houyhnhnms) and ugly beasts (the Yahoos). While the Houyhnhnms are thoughtful and noble creatures, the Yahoos are vile monsters. The Houyhnhnms think that Gulliver is a Yahoo, and there's nothing he can say or do to make them change their opinion. In fact, the more Gulliver listens to the Houyhnhnms, the more he thinks of himself as being no better than a Yahoo. Gulliver thinks very highly of the Houyhnhnms, and he wants to spend the rest of his life with them. But the Houyhnhnms reject him, and he is forced to go home.

In this adventure, Swift shows how it is possible for humans to aspire to live good and kind lives, as the Houyhnhnms do. But, no matter how hard they try, it is human nature to be more like the Yahoos.

However, most readers today would find fault with the Houyhnhnms' seemingly flawless morals. The Houyhnhnms' perfect society relies on the enslavement of the Yahoos, who are treated as objects by the Houyhnhnms. Gulliver (and presumably Swift) doesn't seem to object to this. At the time Swift wrote the book, slavery was common and accepted by many, and so Swift is a product of his time – he does not object to some of the things that modern-day readers would object to.

Timeline of Events

in Swift's life and in 17th- and 18th-century Britain

1667
November 30: Swift is born, in Dublin, Ireland.

1673
Swift begins his education at Kilkenny Grammar School.

1682
April 24: Swift attends Trinity College, Dublin.

1685
February 6: Charles II, King of England, Scotland, and Ireland, dies. Charles's brother, James, becomes King James II of England and Ireland and James VII of Scotland.

1688
December 11: King James is deposed (overthrown) in the Glorious Revolution. Arrival of William and Mary of Orange from Holland.

1689
February 13: William and Mary become King and Queen of England, Scotland, and Ireland.
Swift leaves Trinity College and goes to England where he becomes secretary in the household of Sir William Temple at Moor Park in Surrey.

1690
Swift begins to suffer from Menière's disease—a disease of the inner ear that causes dizziness and nausea (feeling sick).

1692
Swift publishes his first poem—"Ode to the Athenian Society."

1694
December 28: Queen Mary dies.
Swift leaves Temple's household and returns to Ireland to train as a priest.

1695
Swift becomes a priest in the Church of Ireland, and begins work at a church in Kilroot, near Belfast.

1700
Swift moves to Laracor, near Dublin, where he works as a parish priest.

1701
Swift publishes his first political pamphlet.

1702
March 8: King William dies. Anne becomes Queen of England, Scotland, and Ireland.

1704
Swift publishes *A Tale of a Tub, The Battle of the Books,* and *The Mechanical Operation of the Spirit.* His name is not on the books—they are anonymous.

1707
Scotland and England become one country (the Kingdom of Great Britain) when the Act of Union becomes law.

1713
Swift becomes Dean of St. Patrick's Cathedral, Dublin.

1714
August 1: Queen Anne dies. George I becomes King of Great Britain and Ireland.

1720

Swift begins to write *Gulliver's Travels*.

1724

Swift publishes *The Drapier's Letters*. His name is not on the pamphlets—he uses the pseudonym "M. B. Drapier." Swift is celebrated as a hero by the Irish people for challenging England's control over Ireland.

1726

Swift publishes *Gulliver's Travels*. His name is not on the book—he uses the pseudonym "Lemuel Gulliver."

1727

June 11: George I dies. George II becomes King of Great Britain and Ireland.

1730s

Swift's memory starts to fail.

1745

October 19: Swift dies at age 78. He is buried in St. Patrick's Cathedral, Dublin.

"Several Remote Nations"

Gulliver gives us a detailed account of the many places he visits. Although most are fictional countries, Swift gives them real geographical locations. This modern map shows the approximate locations of the lands that Gulliver visits.

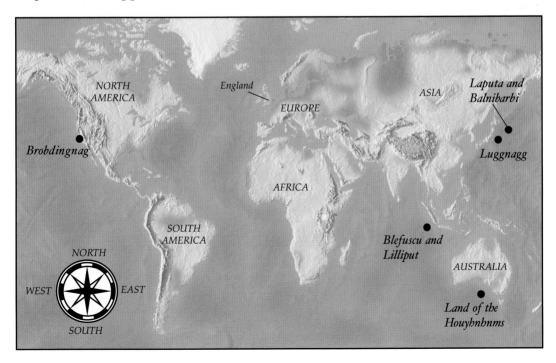

WORKS BY JONATHAN SWIFT

Even today, Jonathan Swift's many works are recognized as great pieces of satire. He wrote poems, political pamphlets, and letters as well as books. Some of these are listed below, including ones that were only published after his death.

1701: *A Discourse on the Contests and Dissentions Between Noble and Commons in Athens and Rome*

1704: *A Tale of a Tub*

1708: *An Argument to Prove That the Abolishing of Christianity in England May, as Things Now Stand, Be Attended with Some Inconveniencies*

1709: *Hints Towards an Essay on Conversation*

1712: *A Proposal for Correcting, Improving, and Ascertaining the English Tongue*

1721: *On English Bubbles*

1724: *The Drapier's Letters to the People of Ireland Against Receiving Wood's Halfpence*

1726: *Travels into Several Remote Nations of the World (Gulliver's Travels)*

1728: *An Account of the Empire of Japan*

1729: *A Modest Proposal for Preventing the Children of Poor People in Ireland from Being a Burden to Their Parents or Country, and for Making Them Beneficial to the Public*

The title page of Swift's 1735 collection of Works. Swift is being thanked by Ireland for his political writings. The Latin motto says "I have made a monument more lasting than brass."

1732: *A Proposal for an Act of Parliament to Pay Off the Debt of the Nation Without Taxing the Subject*

1736: *Reasons Why We Should Not Lower the Coins Now Current in This Kingdom*

1737: *A Proposal for Giving Badges to the Beggars in All the Parishes of Dublin*

1745: *On the Difficulty of Knowing Oneself*

1758: *History of the Last Four Years of the Queen*

1766: *The Journal to Stella*

GULLIVER IN TV AND FILM

Gulliver's Travels has been adapted for the cinema and television many times. It's a very "cinematic" book, with plenty of interesting characters and situations. However, Swift's complicated plot about human nature is much harder to depict, so most filmmakers treat it as a fantasy adventure story, and most of them only choose to adapt the first part of the book (Gulliver's voyage to Lilliput). Here are some film and TV versions of the book:

1902: *Le Voyage de Gulliver à Lilliput et Chez les Géants* (France)
(*The Voyage of Gulliver to Lilliput and the Home of the Giants*)
The very first film of *Gulliver's Travels*, made in black and white and without any sound.

1935: *Noviy Gulliver* (Russia)
(*The New Gulliver*)
A puppet-animated film that linked Gulliver with the communist ideals of Russia. The film showed hard-pressed working-class people triumphing over the ruling class.

1939: *Gulliver's Travels* (USA)
A stop-motion animated film in color with music and songs. Animated films had become very popular, and this film was nominated for an Academy Award (Oscar) for Best Song.

1960: *The 3 Worlds of Gulliver* (USA)
The first live-action adaptation of the book. The makers invented characters of their own, and only adapted Gulliver's voyages to Lilliput and Brobdingnag.

The 3 Worlds of Gulliver, *1960, starring Kerwin Mathews.*

1977: *Gulliver's Travels* (UK)
Only Gulliver's travels to Lilliput were featured in this film.

1982: *Gulliver in Lilliput* (UK)
A mini-series for TV, which concentrated on Gulliver's time in Lilliput.

1996: *Gulliver's Travels* (USA)
A mini-series for TV, notable because it adapted all four of Gulliver's travels.

2005: *Albhutha Dweepu* (Malaysia)
Three hundred dwarves were recruited to play the parts of the Lilliputians.

2010: *Gulliver's Travels* (USA)
A Hollywood movie starring actor Jack Black as Gulliver.

INDEX